Muzzy Mouse'

written and illustrated by
Heather S Buchanan

edited by Nina Filipek
designed by Liz Auger

Published in Great Britain by World International,
an imprint of Egmont Publishing Ltd., Egmont House, PO Box 111,
Great Ducie Street, Manchester M60 3BL.
Printed in Finland. ISBN 0 7498 2276 7

A catalogue record for this book is available from the British Library.

Basil Bat's
branch

N
W E
S

Rumpus Rabbit's
burrow

Muzzy Mouse's
house

Maurice Mole's
hole

Scampa Squirrel's
tree

Henrietta Hedgehog's
log

Buttercup Meadow
stretches from the Deep
Dark Wood in the north,
where Basil Bat and
Scampa Squirrel live, to the
small stream in the south,
where Maurice Mole has
his home.

Henrietta Hedgehog lives
in an old log on the east
side, and Muzzy Mouse's
straw house is under the
hedge to the west. In the
middle of the meadow
lives Rumpus Rabbit.

This is Muzzy's story...

MUZZY Mouse lived at the edge of Buttercup Meadow, where it bordered a field of wheat. She had woven her home out of pieces of straw, and it was tucked away safely under the hedgerow where blackberries grew all summer long.

She could reach out of her window and pluck a blackberry to eat anytime she felt like it. But when she began to long for the taste of something different for supper, she realised she had eaten blackberries, and nothing but blackberries, every day for three whole weeks.

So she set off early on a bright summer morning, with a gingham cloth slung over her shoulder, ready to collect whatever appetising food she could find in Buttercup Meadow.

Muzzy was always a very busy little animal and she liked rushing along at great speed, keeping her eyes open for anything unusual or interesting that might be happening around her. And she loved to be the first to tell the news to her friends Mole, Squirrel, Rabbit, Bat and Hedgehog. Sometimes she would bring back things which she thought would be useful to them.

N ow she hadn't been searching for long before she did discover something quite unusual lying in the grass not far from the stream. It was very large and brightly-coloured. It was actually a rucksack belonging to a boy who was camping in Buttercup Meadow, and who had gone down to the stream to have an early morning swim. It still had the remains of his breakfast in the pockets and, beside it, on the grass, lay an almost-empty milk bottle.

Muzzy could smell the food already. She could hardly believe her luck.

M uzzy was soon scrambling up the front of the rucksack and, finding a pocket that smelled particularly interesting, she squeezed inside.

It contained a bar of fruit and nut chocolate. Half of it had already been eaten, and the heat of the sun was beginning to melt the rest. Muzzy thought it would be wasteful not to eat what remained as quickly as possible. And so she did.

She climbed next into another pocket that held an apple and a small piece of cheese. The apple was just what she needed to clean her teeth, after eating all that chocolate. Then a few bites of cheese finished off the perfect meal with a savoury taste. All she needed now was a drink, and she remembered the almost-empty milk bottle lying in the grass beside the rucksack.

M uzzy was just thinking of climbing down to reach the bottle when she passed another pocket that she had not investigated. She took a quick look, and found, not food, but a little brass chain with a compass on the end. She didn't know what it was, but she felt sure that Maurice Mole would. She didn't realise for a moment that she shouldn't touch it because it might belong to someone else. She pulled it across the grass to the bottle.

With the compass beside her, she looked longingly at the milk in the bottom of the bottle and, without another thought, because she was extremely thirsty, she squeezed inside and slid down until the milk covered her feet. Then she drank and drank.

The little mouse was now very full of food. She began to feel sleepy, as one often does after a good meal. She told herself she deserved a short nap in the cool grass, until she felt energetic enough to carry the compass across the meadow to show Mole.

The sun was higher in the sky now, and it made the glass bottle feel very warm. Muzzy dozed off inside it, even as she was still thinking about climbing out.

The boy came back across the meadow after his swim, picked up his bag, and swung it up on to his shoulder. He forgot about the empty bottle he'd left in the grass, and he didn't notice his old brass compass lying beside it, whilst a fat little mouse slept with his cheese, his chocolate and his apple in her tummy.

M uzzy Mouse felt very unwell, and strangely afraid, when she woke up. As soon as she tried to climb out of the bottle, her paws slipped on the glass and she fell backwards. She squeaked out for help, but no one could hear her.

Maurice Mole was burrowing nearby, as it happened, but he couldn't hear her squeaks. Basil Bat was flying overhead, but he didn't happen to look down at that moment either.

Rumpus Rabbit jogged past in the afternoon, but he was thinking about supper, and he wasn't really watching where he was going.

At last dusk fell, and a beetle and a centipede crept into the bottle beside poor Muzzy, who was quite desperate by now. Although she'd wrapped her gingham cloth around her, she was beginning to feel very cold indeed. She kept on trying to climb out of the bottle but it was just too slippery for her to get a grip.

"I'll never see my friends again," the little mouse whispered to herself sadly.

Luckily, Basil Bat did fly past again that night, and he saw something twinkling on the ground in the moonlight. It was the brass compass.

Swooping down to take a better look, he heard Muzzy's muffled cries from inside the bottle. He could see at once what had happened.

"Hang on, Muzzy," he called to her. "I'll go and fetch the others. We'll get you out, never fear!"

All the animals ran from wherever they were to join Bat on his rescue mission. Maurice Mole had a brilliant idea. He pushed the compass chain into the mouth of the bottle and told Muzzy to grab hold of it with both paws.

Then all her friends pulled on the other end, and Muzzy, who had grown much thinner again as it was a long time since she had eaten anything, popped easily out on to the grass beside them.

Once Muzzy was safely tucked up in her own bed, Maurice sat down and studied the compass that the little mouse had found, and realised with delight that he could use it to find his way when burrowing under Buttercup Meadow. He shortened the chain so he could hang it round his neck.

Meanwhile, the boy went back to look for his lost compass, but sadly didn't find it. He did, however, find the empty milk bottle (with a piece of gingham cloth in it, which surprised him) and took it home, so no other animal was hurt by it again.

M uzzy ate blackberries very gratefully for a while after that. And she was careful never to climb into empty bottles again.

She was proud though, when Mole taught her how to read the compass so she could see that her small house was situated to the west of Buttercup Meadow!

The End

TITLES IN THE BUTTERCUP MEADOW SERIES
BY HEATHER S BUCHANAN